Gordo the Gecko Goes to Ski School

By: Lindsay Frensz

Art by: Nick Charlier & Lindsay Frensz

For my students,
thank you for sharing your imaginations with me
and for the many memorable adventures!
May the clouds always bring you powder days
and the sun keep you warm.
:)

"Good morning, Gordo!" Mama Gecko bent over and licked her son with her long, sticky tongue. "Get up, today you are going to your first ski lesson!"

"Oh no!" groaned Gordo. Geckos like warm weather, and they love to use their sticky hands and feet to climb up things, like trees. Being in the cold and speeding down a mountain did not sound like a good time to Gordo the Gecko.

"You are going to love skiing, Gordo – just you wait and see! Now, get up and eat your breakfast!" Mama Gecko went into the kitchen and poured a bowl of worm and insect cereal for Gordo to eat.

Gordo the Gecko and Mama Gecko packed up the car with all of their winter clothes, skis, ski boots, ski poles for Mama Gecko, helmets, and a thermos of hot cocoa.

"Have a sip of hot cocoa, Gordo, it will warm you up from the inside out and you won't feel so cold in the snow! Careful – blow on it a little, it's hot!" Gordo peered into the dark liquid and blew on it. Then, very carefully, he poked his long tongue into the thermos. The hot cocoa was the most magnificent thing he had ever tasted! It was as if all of his Halloween candy had melted together into this one cup. Gordo licked it once, and then he licked it twice. This day wasn't turning out to be so bad after all! Gordo looked out of the car window as they drove up, up, up the mountain, passing huge pine trees beautifully sprinkled with sparkly white snowflakes.

Finally, Gordo and Mama Gecko arrived at ski school. There were lots of kids Gordo's age, getting dressed for skiing and looking just as nervous as Gordo. There was a penguin girl crying as her Dad tried to jam her feet into her ski boots.

"You're going to love skiing, Peri – just you wait and see!" Peri sniffed loudly, and looked over at the girl next to her.

"I'm Stella." said the girl, a sloth. "At least you only have to wear boots and a helmet." Stella looked miserable as her Grandma covered her in layer after layer of clothes. The poor sloth could barely move! Being a penguin, Peri was used to the snow and the cold. Stella, like Gordo, came from a very warm place, and needed to wear lots of clothes to stay warm in the snow.

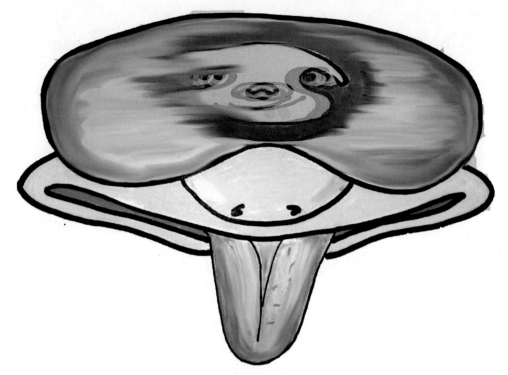

Gordo nervously sat down on the bench next to Stella, and Mama Gecko started helping him dress. First, Gordo put on his long underwear and big, warm ski socks. Next, Gordo put on a warm sweater, and flannel pants. Then, Gordo's mom zipped him up in his black ski bibs and brand new red jacket. Finally, Gordo put on his face mask, goggles, and his helmet, and Mama Gecko helped him put his sticky fingers into some fluffy blue mittens. Stella the Sloth laughed at Gordo,

"You look like a super hero!" She made a funny face at her reflection in Gordo's goggles.

"So do you!" giggled Gordo.

Once the children dressed, they gathered in a room to wait for their ski instructor.

"Do you think he will be big and fat and have a beard like Santa Claus?" wondered Peter the Porcupine.

"Will she make us write things on the chalkboard, like at regular school?" Riley the Rabbit asked aloud. Before long, their questions were answered, and a polar bear with a big smile appeared.

"Hi guys! I'm Coach Chris. I'll be teaching you how to do the coolest thing ever today – ski down a mountain! But first, I want to learn about you guys. Why don't you all tell me your name, and what you like to do." Stella, who was the least shy of the group, spoke up first,

"I'm Stella the Sloth, and I like to climb trees!" Stella grinned.

"That's great!" said Coach Chris, "After a little practice, we can ski through the trees – how does that sound?" Stella beamed.

"How about you?" Coach Chris pointed at Riley.

"I'm Riley the Rabbit, and I like to run fast."

"Super! After a little practice, you will be able to ski even faster than you run!"

"I like the sound of that!" Boom, boom boom! Riley thumped his ski boots excitedly on the floor.

"And you, Ms. Penguin?" Even though Coach Chris seemed really nice, Peri still felt shy.

"I'm Peri. The penguin." Peri spoke so softly the group could barely hear her, but Coach Chris did.

"Great to meet you, Peri! You are going to be a great leader today, since you already know all about snow! What do you like to do, Peri?" Peri looked at her feet, all squashed into her ski boots.

"I'm not sure I'll be much of a skier. I like to do art."

"That's perfect!" exclaimed Coach Chris, "Did you know that fresh snow is just like a giant piece of paper, and our skis work like pencils? When we ski around, we make beautiful designs in the snow! I can't wait to see your artwork today!" Peri blushed, and smiled a little, before looking back at her feet. "And how about you..." Coach Chris looked over at the porcupine and tried not to laugh at the quills poking out of his jacket. Gordo scooted a little bit further away from his prickly classmate. "Name's Peter. I'm a singer in a band."

"Right on, Peter! Having a loud voice is important in the mountains. You can be our team's safety guy – whenever somebody falls, you cry 'Wipeout!' And the group will know to stop and wait. Finally..." Coach Chris's gaze fell upon Gordo, "I can't tell what animal you are, superhero!"

"I'm Gordo the Gecko. I like to eat bugs and sit in the sun."

"Well, when you are high up in the mountains, like we are now, you are about as close to the sun as you can get on planet Earth. There aren't many bugs in the snow, but we can pretend to catch them when we ski. And, we will have snack time later in the day. Nobody can ski when they're hungry!"

The group headed out onto the snow. Gordo stuck out his long, sticky tongue to catch a falling snowflake. Peter made a snowball and took a bite out of it. Though the snow was cold, the bundled up creatures were toasty warm. Everyone could tell that Peri had been in the snow before when she immediately dove onto the snow and slid on her belly all the way to where Coach Chris was waiting.

"Wow! Cool slide, Peri!" yelled Riley as he tried to do the same thing. Riley dove face-first into the fresh snow and sunk so deeply, only his fluffy cotton-tail was visible above the snow. Peri had to stifle a small giggle.

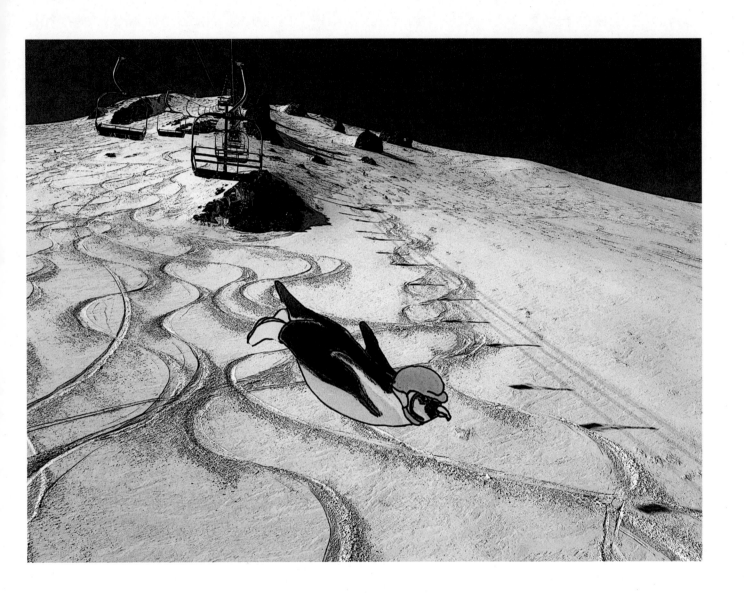

Coach Chris taught the kids how to put on their skis and slide around on the flat ground. Then, he taught them how to brake by moving their feet and plowing the snow. It was time to ski downhill and practice stopping!

Stella went down the hill first, with her skis pointed in the shape of an arrow. She went very very slowly, typical of a sloth, and came to a gentle stop at the bottom as she spread her legs and made her arrow bigger.

"Nicely done, Stella!" called Coach Chris, "Alright, you're up Riley!" Unlike Stella the Sloth, Riley the Rabbit loves speed. Riley kept his

skis pointed straight, like the number 11. Whooosh! Riley rocketed down the hill, and forgot how to s t o p ! "MAKE YOUR WEDGE! LIKE A SLICE OF PIZZA!" Coach Chris yelled from the top of the hill, but Riley was going too fast to hear him. He finally ran into a big pile of snow and made a rabbit-shaped imprint, ears and all.

"Wipeouuutttt!!!!" sang

Peter the Porcupine.

"Dude! That was awesome!" the group could hear Riley's muffled voice as he climbed out of the snow pile.

"Remember your stopping shape?" Coach Chris reminded Riley how to turn his feet to slow down.

"Pshaw. Who needs to slow down?!" Riley laughed as he hopped back to the group, shaking off his cotton-tail.

Peter the Porcupine was next. He took a deep breath, slid his skis into the wedge, and smoothly glided to the bottom of the slope, where he spread his legs even wider, and came to a stop.

"Perfect form, Peter!" Coach Chris was proud of his students. Peri went next, and though she desperately wanted to perform her famous penguin-slide down the slope, she followed Coach Chris's instructions and turned her feet into the shape of an arrow pointing down the hill. At the bottom, instead of making her arrow wider, Peri pointed both of her toes to the right. She had made a right-hand turn!

"Wow, Peri! You just taught yourself how to turn! And look at the pretty rainbow shape you made in the snow!" Peri looked back and smiled, maybe artists could be skiers!

Finally, it was Gordo's turn. Gordo had been watching his classmates carefully, but still felt a bit nervous. His skis felt so big on his little legs.

"You're up, Gordo! Whenever you're ready!" called out Coach Chris. Gordo looked down the hill, and then down at his skis. He tried to slide them into the triangle shape, but the edges of his skis stuck in the snow, and he ended up with one foot turned and the other foot pointed straight down the slope. Before he was ready, all of his foot movement caused Gordo to start sliding downhill!

"Woooaaahhhhh!!!!" Gordo closed his eyes and leaned backwards, dragging his tail on the snow to try to keep himself from falling. One of Gordo's skis slid one way, and the other ski went the other way. Both of Gordo's arms started flailing in circles. "Wooaahhhh!!!!" Gordo cried out again as he lost complete control of his body. BOOM!

"Wipeouuutttttt!" sang Peter the Porcupine.

Gordo sat up and shook his head, his eyeballs were spinning in circles. He looked around, one ski was laying on the snow way above him, and the other way below him. Coach Chris was standing right next to him, offering his hand.

"Hey, you okay, Gordo?"

"I....guess so." Gordo felt his arms and legs. Everything seemed to be alright.

"Let me help you up." Coach Chris easily lifted Gordo to his feet, and quickly collected his skis. "That was a great try! You really moved your feet well – that's a hard thing to do! Now, all you have to do is slow it down."

"I don't want to try again. I don't think skiing is for Geckos." Gordo the Gecko licked some cold snow off of his lips with his long, sticky tongue. He shivered, and snow fell out of his helmet. Gordo looked down at the sparkling white snow.

"Learning new things can be tough, and sometimes you have to fall down a few times before you figure it out. Remember when you learned to ride a bike? You probably fell once or twice, but it was worth it, because riding a bike gives you freedom to go so many places! Skiing gives you freedom to explore an entire mountain, and play outside even when it's stormy. I know the snow seems cold and unwelcoming to you, but maybe you just have to look at it a little bit closer."

"What do you mean?" asked Gordo. Without realizing it, Gordo was allowing Coach Chris to help him step back into his skis.

"See how the snow sparkles? The snow only sparkles like that when the sun is shining bright. Each snowflake acts like a mirror, reflecting the sun which brings you so much warmth and joy. The snowflakes are like millions of tiny suns below your feet, shining up on you." Gordo looked at the snow a little bit closer. Coach Chris was right, Gordo could feel the warmth reflecting off of the cold snowflakes.

"It is beautiful," Gordo admitted.

"Whaddaya say we try it one more time, Gordo? Now you know what it's going to be like – it will be easier this time, I promise."

"Well…." Gordo still wasn't quite sure, but Coach Chris's smile was very encouraging. "Okay, I guess." Coach Chris helped Gordo to the top of the hill, and stood in front of him as he arranged his skis into the shape of a slice of pizza. Gordo liked pizza. Especially if it was covered in wriggling mealworms. Delicious!

"Alright Gordo, that looks great! Don't move so much now, just stay strong in this position. When you want to stop, slowly slide your feet into a bigger slice of pizza." Gordo nodded, and focused his gaze downhill. Out of the corner of his eye, he saw millions of sparkling snowflakes. Gordo leaned forward, and began to pick up speed. He slid a little bit faster, and then a little bit faster. Just as his tail began to sway nervously, Gordo remembered what he was supposed to do. He slid his feet carefully into a bigger slice of pizza, and suddenly, he was slowing down! Gordo slid his feet a little bit wider still, and came to a smooth stop at the bottom of the slope.

"Woohoo!" cried the other children from the top of the hill.

"Wow!" exclaimed Coach Chris, "That looked great, Gordo! Did you guys all see that?" Coach Chris turned to the rest of the class, "That's exactly what stopping is supposed to look like!" Gordo smiled. Strangely, even though he was standing in the snow, he felt very, very warm inside.

The children took turns skiing a few more times, and everyone did a wonderful job. They became very good at stopping, and even learned how to turn! At the end of the day, Mama Gecko came to pick up Gordo.

"Well?" Mama Gecko asked.

"I LOVE SKIING!" Gordo cried, "Can we please come back tomorrow?!"

About the Author

Lindsay Frensz is a ski instructor at Mammoth Mountain. The best part about being a ski instructor is sharing the magic of the mountain with others. Every day on the mountain is beautiful and unique, and Lindsay loves to help people discover that beauty by teaching them how to go out and explore the mountain using skis as their transportation. Lindsay also really loves animals, which is why she made all of the characters in the book animals. She usually teaches human beings how to ski, and is sorry to say she has never had an opportunity to play in the snow with a penguin.

Made in the USA
Monee, IL
09 January 2023

24979434R00017